Dear Parents:

Congratulations! Your child is taking the first steps on an exciting journey. The destination? Independent reading!

STEP INTO READING® will help your child get there. The program offers five steps to reading success. Each step includes fun stories and colorful art or photographs. In addition to original fiction and books with favorite characters, there are Step into Reading Non-Fiction Readers, Phonics Readers and Boxed Sets, Sticker Readers, and Comic Readers—a complete literacy program with something to interest every child.

Learning to Read, Step by Step!

Ready to Read   Preschool–Kindergarten
• big type and easy words • rhyme and rhythm • picture clues
For children who know the alphabet and are eager to begin reading.

Reading with Help   Preschool–Grade 1
• basic vocabulary • short sentences • simple stories
For children who recognize familiar words and sound out new words with help.

Reading on Your Own   Grades 1–3
• engaging characters • easy-to-follow plots • popular topics
For children who are ready to read on their own.

Reading Paragraphs   Grades 2–3
• challenging vocabulary • short paragraphs • exciting stories
For newly independent readers who read simple sentences with confidence.

Ready for Chapters   Grades 2–4
• chapters • longer paragraphs • full-color art
For children who want to take the plunge into chapter books but still like colorful pictures.

STEP INTO READING® is designed to give every child a successful reading experience. The grade levels are only guides; children will progress through the steps at their own speed, developing confidence in their reading.

Remember, a lifetime love of reading starts with a single step!

Visit us on the Web!
StepIntoReading.com
randomhousekids.com

Educators and librarians, for a variety of teaching tools, visit us at RHTeachersLibrarians.com

ISBN 978-1-101-93704-4 (trade) — ISBN 978-1-101-93705-1 (lib. bdg.)

Printed in the United States of America

10 9 8 7 6 5 4 3

nickelodeon

SHiMMER
and
Shine™

Movie Night Magic!

by Mary Tillworth

illustrated by Dave Aikins

Random House 🏠 New York

It is movie night!
Leah and Zac
want to watch
The Dragon Princess.

Leah makes popcorn.

Zac blows up

their chairs.

The popcorn burns.
Zac's puppy, Rocket,
chews a hole in a chair.
The TV will not play!

Zac goes home
to fix the chair.
Leah calls for her genies,
Shimmer and Shine!

Shimmer and Shine
grant Leah
three wishes.
First, Leah wishes
for more popcorn.

Pop! Pop! Pop!
Popcorn fills
the room!

Shimmer and Shine
made a mistake.
But it is okay.

For her second wish,

Leah wants to play

The Dragon Princess.

The genies think
Leah wants to *be*
a princess.

They change her house
into a castle.
Then they turn her
into a princess.

Oh, no! A dragon!
It breathes
green smoke.

Leah wishes for
the dragon to stop
breathing smoke.
That is her last wish!

Now the dragon hiccups
green bubbles.

The dragon is hungry.

It wants to eat

Leah's house!

Leah tells the dragon
to eat popcorn!

The dragon eats
all the popcorn.
It flies away!

Zac comes back.
He fixes the chair
with popcorn!
He thinks the castle
is a great movie set.

Leah plays the princess.
Zac plays the knight.
Zac's puppy
plays the dragon.

It is the best
movie night ever!

Leah thanks
Shimmer and Shine
for another day when
mistakes came out great!